It's Cloudy!

Julie Richards

Smart Apple Media

Smart Apple Media
1980 Lookout Drive
North Mankato
Minnesota 56003

Library of Congress Cataloging-in-Publication Data

Richards, Julie.
It's cloudy! / by Julie Richards.
p. cm. — (How's the weather?)
Includes bibliographical references and index.
ISBN 1-58340-537-2 (alk. paper)
1. Clouds—Juvenile literature. [1. Clouds. 2. Weather.] I. Title.
QC921.35.R53 2004
551.57'6—dc22   2003070412

First Edition
9 8 7 6 5 4 3 2 1

First published in 2004 by
MACMILLAN EDUCATION AUSTRALIA PTY LTD
627 Chapel Street, South Yarra 3141

Associated companies and representatives throughout the world.

Copyright © Julie Richards 2004

Edited by Vanessa Lanaway
Page layout by Domenic Lauricella
Illustrations by Melissa Webb
Photo research by Legend Images

Printed in China

Acknowledgements
The author and the publisher are grateful to the following for permission to reproduce copyright material:

Cover photograph: boy looking at clouds, courtesy of Photolibrary.com/Index Stock

HoaQui/Auscape, p. 22; F. Lechenet—Explorer/Auscape, p. 15; C. Monteath—Explorer/Auscape, p. 7; Reg Morrison/Auscape, p. 8; Richard Packwood—OSF/Auscape, p. 23; BrandX Pictures, p. 10; Corbis Digital Stock, p. 18; Digital Vision, pp. 14, 20, 21, 27; Getty Images/Photodisc Blue, p. 17 (bottom); Getty Images/Taxi, p. 11; Len Stewart/Lochman Transparencies, p. 26; Pelusey Photography, p. 28; Photodisc, pp. 4, 5, 6, 9, 29; Photolibrary.com/Index Stock, pp. 1, 25; Photolibrary.com/SPL, p. 19; Sporting Images, p. 30; Stockbyte, pp. 16 (both), 17 (top).

While every care has been taken to trace and acknowledge copyright, the publisher tenders their apologies for any accidental infringement where copyright has proved untraceable. Where the attempt has been unsuccessful, the publisher welcomes information that would redress the situation.

Please note
At the time of printing, the Internet addresses appearing in this book were correct. Owing to the dynamic nature of the Internet, however, we cannot guarantee that all these addresses will remain correct.

Contents

How's the Weather?

Have you noticed how the weather always changes? You might feel hot sunshine or a cold wind, see clouds gathering or hear thunder. Weather changes from day to day and **season** to season.

These children are having fun outside on a cloudy day.

Most places have cloudy as well as clear weather.

The weather varies from place to place, too. Some places have cloudy skies that bring lots of rain. Deserts have mostly clear skies and are very dry. How's the weather where you live?

Clouds

Clouds are made of millions of tiny water drops and ice **crystals** that stick together. The different shapes and patterns made by clouds can tell us what kind of weather might be coming.

These clouds may bring a change of weather in a few days.

The shape of these clouds tells us that strong winds may be coming.

Some clouds are thick, grey, and stormy. Others might be long and thin like a horse's tail, or look like strange spaceships! Sometimes the cloud is just like a thick blanket spread across the sky.

7

A Cloudy Day

On rainy days, heavy rain clouds can block out the sun all day. A hot, sticky day often ends with black storm clouds that bring lightning and thunder.

These storm clouds are bringing a change of weather after a sunny day.

These clouds are carrying rain across the sky.

The wind blows clouds across the sky. A cloud might bring a little burst of rain called a shower. It soon passes and the sun shines again.

Cloudy Day Gear

If it's a cloudy day, the weather can turn cold and wet. Keep a warm jumper, a raincoat, and rubber boots handy. This gear will keep you warm and dry while you have fun outside.

Warm clothes will keep you warm if the weather turns cold.

In some places clouds can bring
heavy rain, even on hot days.

In some places cloudy days can be hot and
sticky. When huge black clouds roll in, they
bring cool, refreshing rain.

Where Do Clouds Come From?

Clouds are part of the **water cycle**, which uses water again and again.

Clouds are made of water drops.

Sun

4 The water drops join together to form clouds.

3 As it rises, the water vapor cools and turns back into water drops.

1 Sunshine turns water into a gas called water vapor.

2 Water vapor rises into the air.

If the air inside a cloud is very cold, the water drops freeze and turn into **hailstones** or snowflakes.

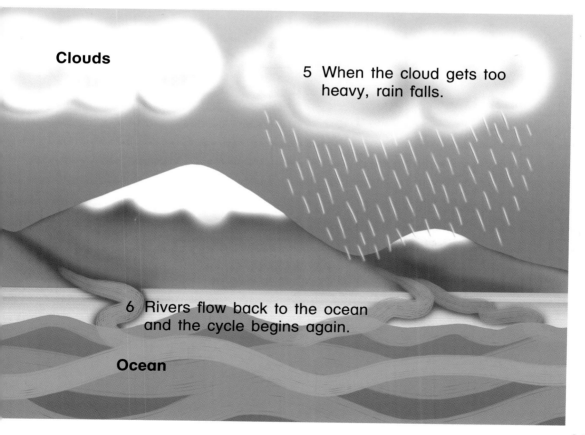

Clouds

5 When the cloud gets too heavy, rain falls.

6 Rivers flow back to the ocean and the cycle begins again.

Ocean

Cloudy Seasons

Clouds in spring bring rain that helps plants grow. In winter, the clouds sometimes bring snow. Summer thunderclouds come at the end of a hot, sticky day.

Clouds bring rain that helps plants to grow.

This girl is walking through heavy rain during the wet season.

Some places only have a wet season and a dry season. During the wet season, powerful winds, called monsoons, push huge rain clouds across the sky nearly every day. Rain can pour down for days at a time.

Reading Clouds

Different clouds bring different kinds of weather. The shapes and patterns clouds make tell us what kind of weather might come.

Cumulus clouds are small, white, and fluffy. They are seen during fine weather.

Cirrus clouds are feathery and float very high in the sky. They warn that the weather will change during the next few days.

Cumulonimbus clouds are towering clouds that bring ferocious thunderstorms.

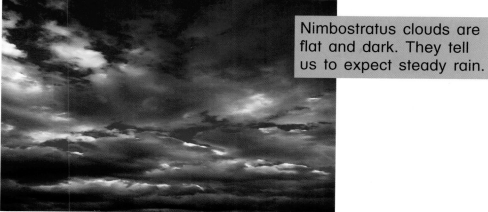

Nimbostratus clouds are flat and dark. They tell us to expect steady rain.

Clouds are moved about by the wind. They travel as part of a **weather system**. Different weather systems have different clouds, depending on the type of weather they bring.

17

We Need Clouds

People, plants, and animals need water to live.
Clouds bring rain and snow that fills oceans
and rivers. This gives people and animals
fresh drinking water, and helps plants grow.

Without clouds, these animals
would have no drinking water.

A big storm like this can ruin crops.

Nearly all our food comes from farms. **Crops** need rain to grow, but big storms can ruin them. Farmers watch the clouds to see if rain or storms are coming. If clouds warn that storms are coming, farmers might **harvest** their crops early.

Thick Clouds

Sometimes thick clouds act like curtains and block the sun's light and warmth. When this happens, it takes longer for snow to melt and puddles to dry up.

The sun is hidden behind these clouds.

Deserts heat up and cool down very quickly because they have no clouds.

On a warm day, clouds can act like a blanket and stop heat from escaping. Deserts usually have no clouds. They heat up quickly during the day and cool down quickly at night.

21

Dangerous Clouds

Sometimes clouds mix with dirty air, called pollution. This is caused by chemicals in the air from cars, factories, and power stations. Many countries are passing laws to stop these chemicals from being sent into the air.

Dirty air can look like a brown cloud.

These trees have been poisoned by acid rain.

The chemicals mix with water drops and ice crystals inside clouds. The poisoned water drops and ice crystals fall as acid rain or acid snow. This can kill plants and poison water so animals cannot drink it.

Forecasting Clouds

Scientists who **forecast** weather are called meteorologists. They use computers and look at **satellite** photos to find different kinds of clouds. This information is used to forecast weather.

Symbols on weather maps show us what kind of weather is coming.

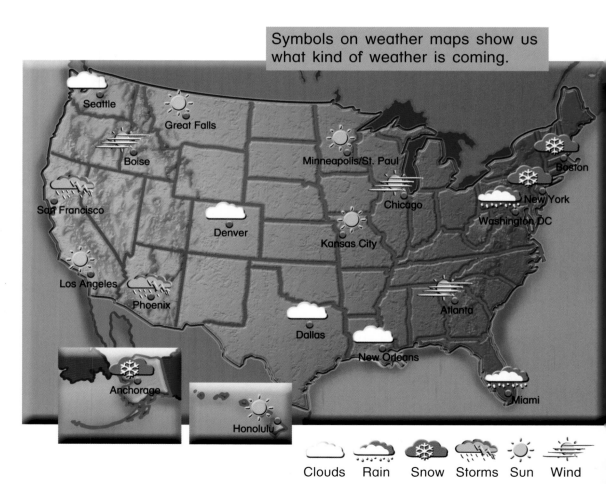

Seattle
Great Falls
Boise
Minneapolis/St. Paul
San Francisco
Chicago
Denver
New York
Washington DC
Kansas City
Los Angeles
Phoenix
Atlanta
Dallas
New Orleans
Anchorage
Miami
Honolulu
Boston

Clouds Rain Snow Storms Sun Wind

This radar tower helps us to find out what is inside clouds.

Meteorologists use **radar** to look at clouds. Radar tells them if there are raindrops and hailstones inside clouds. Meteorologists can follow a storm with radar and warn people if the storm might become dangerous.

25

Mist and Fog

Mist is a kind of cloud that forms above the ground. When warm, **moist** air moves across cold ground, some of the water vapor in it changes into water drops. The water drops collect together to become a mist.

Mist is a kind of cloud that has formed near the ground.

This car is almost completely hidden by fog.

Fog is a very thick mist that can be hard to see through. Some cars have special foglights that can shine through fog. Ships hidden in fog use a foghorn to warn other ships they are nearby.

Cloudy Sayings

People use weather sayings and words to describe everyday things.

Every cloud has a silver lining.
Some people believe that for every bad thing that happens, good things happen too. We just have to look for them.

A face like a thundercloud.
This means that someone looks very unhappy. People say that the angry look on their face looks like a thundercloud.

This cloud has a silver lining.

Weather Wonders

Did you know?

⭐ The tallest clouds are cumulonimbus clouds. They can be as tall as 39 of the world's tallest skyscrapers stacked on top of one another.

⭐ In 1959, pilot William Rankin parachuted out of his aircraft in the middle of a thundercloud. He was tossed about by ferocious winds and pelted by hailstones. The lightning was so bright that he had to close his eyes, and the thunder shook his body. Rankin spent 40 minutes inside the thundercloud and escaped with just a few bruises.

Try This!

Ask a parent or teacher for help.

Make a cloud

✪ Place ice in a metal dish and let it stand until the dish is very cold.

✪ Place about one inch (2 cm) of warm water in a large jar.

✪ Put the metal dish over the top of the jar and watch.

✪ Look near the top of the jar. What has happened?

Water vapor from the warm water rose to the top, where the cold air turned it back into water drops. The water drops joined together to make a "cloud."

Glossary

crops	plants grown for food
crystals	tiny pieces of ice
forecast	to know what kind of weather is coming
hailstones	frozen raindrops
harvest	to cut and gather ripened crops
moist	air that is filled with water drops or water vapor
radar	a way of looking at faraway objects
satellite	a small spacecraft that circles Earth and takes photographs
season	a part of the year that has its own kind of weather
water cycle	the way water is used again and again
weather system	a group of clouds traveling together that bring a certain kind of weather

Index

Weather on the Web

Here are some Web sites that you might like to look at:
http://www.pals.iastate.edu/carlson/main.html
http://www.wildwildweather.com/clouds.htm

DATE DUE

FEB 1 1 2011		
FEB 2 4 2011		

Demco